Big Bird's Bedtime Story

A Random House PICTUREBACK®

On *Sesame Street,* Luis is played by Emilio Delgado
and David is played by Northern Calloway.

Library of Congress Cataloging-in-Publication Data:
Wetzel, Rick. Big Bird's bedtime story. (Random House pictureback) SUMMARY: Luis tells Big Bird a bedtime story about an enormous egg and the surprise it contained when it hatched. [1. Eggs—Fiction. 2. Puppets—Fiction] I. Swanson, Maggie. II. Henson, Jim. III. Children's Television Workshop. IV. Title. PZ7.W535Bi 1987 [E] 87-4764 ISBN: 0-394-89126-0 (trade); 0-394-99126-5 (lib. bdg.) Manufactured in the United States of America   27 28 29 30

Big Bird's Bedtime Story

By Rick Wetzel
and
Maggie Swanson

**FEATURING JIM HENSON'S
SESAME STREET MUPPETS**

Random House/Children's Television Workshop

One summer evening on Sesame
Street, Luis came by when Big Bird
was getting ready for bed. He tucked
Big Bird into his nest.

"I am not sleepy yet," said Big
Bird. "Will you tell me a story,
Luis?"

"Sure, Big Bird," said Luis. "What
kind of story would you like?"

Big Bird thought for a minute.
"Tell me a story about *me*," he said.

"All right, Big Bird. Listen carefully. This story starts on the day of the special delivery to Mr. Hooper's store," began Luis.

Early one morning while everyone was still sound asleep, Sam's Dairy Farm truck made its daily delivery to Hooper's Store. But there was something different, something special about this delivery. Instead of ten boxes of eggs, the truck left one big box with one enormous egg in it.

When David opened the store, Ernie and Grover
helped him put the milk into the store's refrigerator.
But none of them knew what to do with the big egg.

"I didn't order this egg," said David. "Why, it won't even fit into the refrigerator!"

"Don't worry, David," said Ernie. "We'll take care of the egg."

And that's just what they did. They got Bert, Cookie Monster, and Telly Monster to help them. First they gathered twigs in the park and straw from crates that a movers' van had left behind. Then they built a big nest for the egg.

"Was the nest like mine, Luis?"
asked Big Bird.
"Yes," answered Luis. "It was
exactly like yours, Big Bird."

When the nest was finished, they carefully lifted the big egg into its new home.

"Whew, that was hard work," said Grover.

"We aren't done yet," said Bert. "Now we need to keep the egg warm so that it will hatch."

"What does *hatch* mean?" asked Telly.

"That is when the egg breaks and whoever is inside it is born!" explained Bert.

"Me keep big egg warm!" yelled Cookie Monster. He climbed into the nest.

"Wait a minute!" cried Grover. "Be careful, Cookie. You might break the egg. We can keep this eggy warm with my cute, cuddly blanket."

And that's just what they did.

"Hey, Bert, old buddy, that's the biggest pigeon egg I've ever seen," Ernie said, laughing.

"Don't be silly, Ernie," said Bert. "That's much too big to be a pigeon egg. It might be a dinosaur egg. I saw one just like that at the museum."

"I hope it is a hippopotamus egg," said Telly Monster.
"Little baby hippos do not come from eggs. They come from big mommy hippos," said Grover smartly. "But dragons come from eggs. Do you think it is a dragon?"

Big Bird broke into Luis's story. He wanted to know what *was* in that egg.

"Was it my friend Mr. Snuffle-upagus?" asked Big Bird.

Luis smiled. "No, Big Bird. And dragons aren't real and there haven't been any dinosaurs on earth for millions of years. Lots of different birds, and even turtles, come from eggs. But the egg in my story," he said, "is the biggest egg in the world."

No one wanted to leave the egg, but soon it was time for playgroup.

"Do not be afraid," said Grover to the egg. "We will be back soon. Please do not hatch until we come back."

They all said good-bye to the egg.

When playgroup was over, they all rushed back to the
nest. They told the egg all about what they had done at
playgroup. Ernie showed the egg the picture he had
painted.

After dinner they hurried back to the nest. The egg was exactly the same as before.

"I wish that egg would wake up and hatch," said Ernie.

Oscar the Grouch popped his head out of his garbage can. "I know how to wake up that crummy old egg! Heh-heh! I'll play some of my favorite grouch music!" And that's just what he did.

"Stop that horrible noise!" shouted Bert. "The egg needs to sleep. And so do I."

It was past their bedtime, so
they all went home.
"Good night," said Bert.
"Good night," said Ernie.

"Sleep tight, eggy," said
Grover as he tucked in the egg.
"See you in the morning,"
said Telly.

"Luis! I thought this story was going to be about *me*," said Big Bird sleepily.

"Don't fall asleep now, Big Bird. Listen—we're coming to the good part," said Luis.

The next morning Grover was the first one awake. He couldn't wait to see if the egg had hatched. He tiptoed up to the nest and peeked inside.

"Come and look, everybody!" shouted Grover.

Telly Monster, Cookie Monster, Ernie, and Bert all came running to the nest. Even Oscar the Grouch couldn't wait to see what the noise was all about.

There were four large cracks in the egg, and a pointy little beak was just poking through the shell.

"Peck, peck," said the egg.

"Oh, my goodness," said Grover. "It is hatching!"

Then the egg broke open at last. And they couldn't believe what they saw.

"Can you guess who hatched from the big egg in the nest?" Luis asked Big Bird.
But Big Bird was sound asleep.